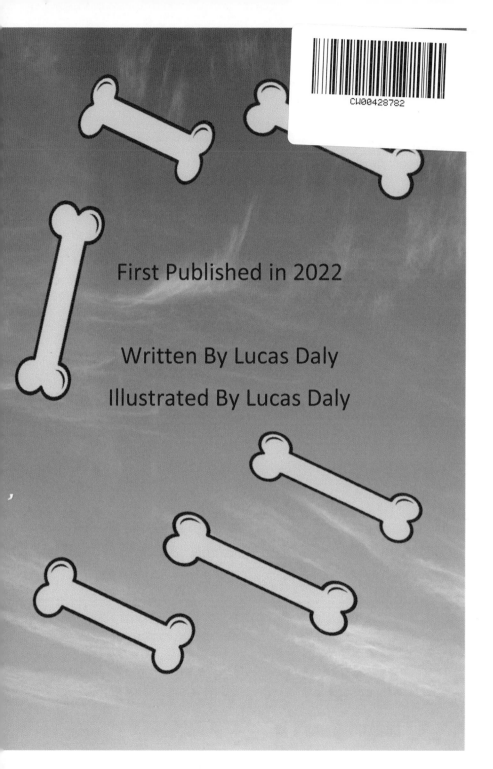

First Published in 2022

Written By Lucas Daly

Illustrated By Lucas Daly

CW00428782

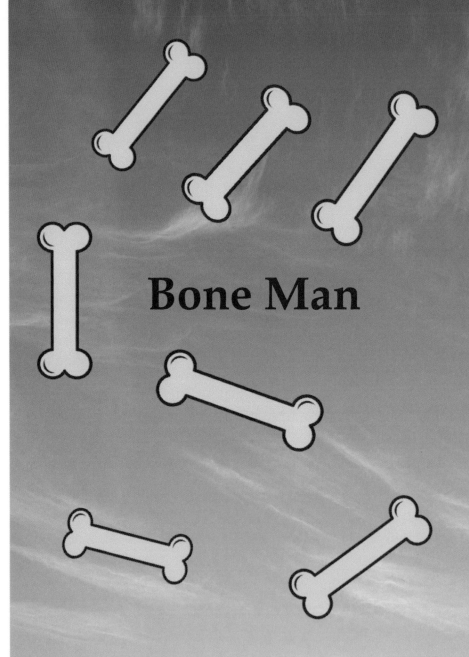

Bone Man

One day long ago there was a robber on the loose. But...

Bone Man came to the rescue!

The robber saw Bone Man, so it ran the opposite way, but when he ran there, he saw there was police there. But ...

The robber just jumped over the police and ran away.

"What ya do that for?" said Bone Man.

Finally, Bone Man captured the robber by using one of his funky bones.

A new villain has raised, one looking for trouble; Big trouble.

The villain was called 'Manchato Santaino'.

He built a robot to try to stop Bone Man.

Manchato Santaino done his evil laugh, HA HA HA.

"Bone Man will never get me."

Manchato Santaino went to Bone
Man's city destroying everything.

Manchato Santaino and his robot went to Bone Man.

Bone Man threw a lot of funky bones, but they missed.

How could Bone Man win?

Bone Man got closer and closer to the robot.

Bone Man took some more Bones off himself throwing them at the robot destroying it.

Manchato Santaino had funky stuff too, a dog.

"Oh, what is this?" he laughed.

"Bone Man it's a dog, go get him." Said Manchato Santaino to the dog.

Bone Man threw a funky bone at the dog and the dog exploded.

Manchato Santaino run away, Bone Man saved the city.

How to draw Bone Man

Bone Man
and
the secrets
of the world

Bone Man was walking in Bone Man city, until he looked to his right.

Standing their looking him right in the eye was Manchato Santaino.

Manchato Santaino jumped down onto Bone Man and opened the sewer door that was next to him, and pushed Bone Man in it.

Bone Man fell for one hour, until

he landed in the sewers with a bump.

Bone man wandered where he was,
but then he heard a whistle.

"Sounds like Manchato Santaino's
whistle" Bone Man said to himself.

But Manchato Santaino was nowhere
to be seen. Was it a trick?

Then right there, in front of him, he
saw a snake.

"Run" Bone Man said and when he was running, he realised that there was nobody else there but him and the snake.

Soon his boney detector rang, the book was close.

Bone Man tried running through the tunnels of the sewers to avoid the snake.

How can Bone Man get away?

Bone Man kept on running and screamed and screamed before thinking of an idea.

He saw that the snake was very tired.

He opened the snake's mouth and looked inside it.

There it was, right in front of him.

The book

THE SECRETS OF THE WORLD

Bone Man read the book finding out lots of things, he even found out how to do magic.

How to increase the size of his funky bones.

How to make them follow people around corners.

To come away and then boomerang back to them.

Bone Man was stronger than ever.

Now how to get out of here?

Using the magic Bone Man had just learnt, he stretched one of his funky bones up the wall of the sewers to one of the openings and climbed out.

Bone Man was free to help fight against evil again.

The End

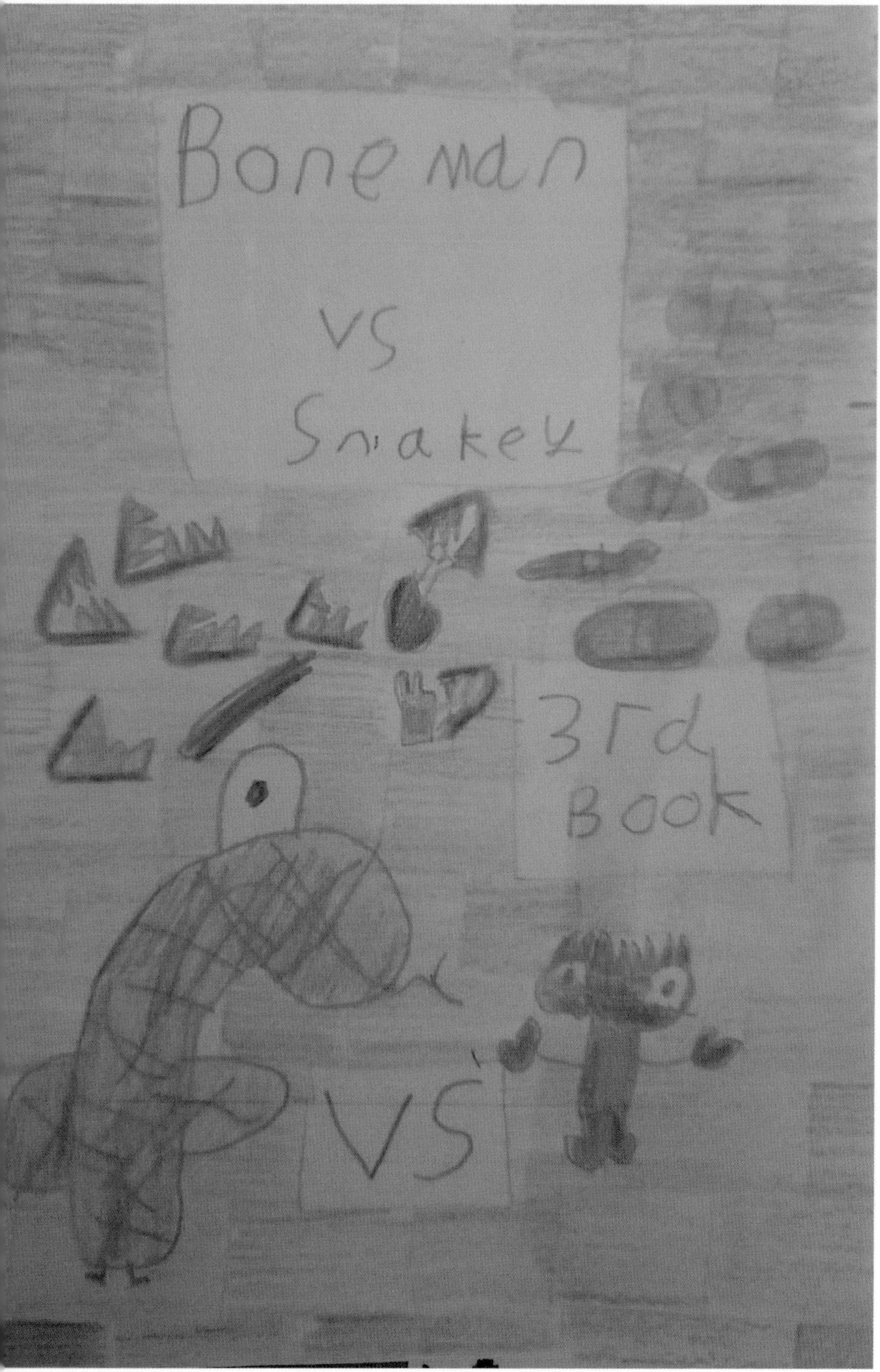
Boneman
VS
Snakey
3rd
Book
VS

BONE MAN VS SNAKEY

Bone Man was getting Manchato
Santaino until, a portal appeared.

Bone Man jumped into the portal.

Snakey was playing football until another portal appeared.

Snakey jumped into the portal.

The portal took the two of them to a dark hall. Bone Man looked behind him, the portal had disappeared.

Realising they weren't alone; they got their weapons ready.

Looking around the hall getting scared more by the minute, until they saw each other.

Bone Man threw a lot of funky bones at Snakey, who ran to avoid them carried by his tiny legs.

Snakey attempted to get close to Bone Man and get him with his special power.

TO EAT BONE MAN!!!

Bone Man threw another bone towards Snakey. Snakey opened his mouth and ate the bone. "Yum" Snakey said.

Bone Man moved quickly to avoid Snakey, but after some time Snakey knocked Bone Man down using his tail.

Was this the end for Bone Man?

Bone man recovered to his feet grabbing Snakey by the tail.

Avoiding his head, Bone man threw Snakey around in circles above his head throwing him against the wall.

Who was going to win the fight?

Suddenly Bone Man remembered the book and the magic.

Throwing a funky bone towards Snakey he shouts "boomerang".

The bone turned away from snakey, tricking him, before turning back and knocking him down.

Throwing a second bone yelling "enlarge" just as snakey opened his mouth to eat it.

The bone got stuck in Snakey's mouth leaving it wide open.

The fight continued into the night, bones flying and Snakey attacking with all parts of his body.

After some time, Bone Man figured out that Snakey wasn't a villain after all, in fact he was a superhero just like him.

They were both good guys.

Bone Man and Snakey decided to join forces and work together to defeat evil.

All about the Author

Lucas Daly was born in England and enjoyed reading from a young age. Shortly after his sixth birthday, he sat down and wrote these books being inspired by Dav Pilkey; who's books he had been reading at the time. Lucas also enjoys a number of different sports including Football, Tennis and Swimming as well as playing with Lego, word games and Number games.

Printed in Great Britain
by Amazon